TENDERFOOT

Story by
Toby and Brad Bluth

Illustrations by
Toby Bluth

Ideals Publishing Corp.
Nashville, Tennessee

ISBN 0-8249-8088-3

Once there were three buddies, a duck named Dickie, a rabbit named Jack, and a monkey called Bobo. They were the best of friends and as close as brothers.

The duck was a dapper sort of kid and a little conceited, but this was only because he was aware of his own startling good looks. The rabbit, on the other hand, relied less on his good looks and more on his brain. The monkey, by contrast, was neither conceited nor brainy. He moved by instinct. One summer, the buddies joined a scout troop.

This night, the troop met to prepare for a
camping trip in the wilderness, far away from
the city. The buddies listened intently as
scoutmaster Old Dog and his assistant, Trusty

Beaver, checked the list of supplies. If there's
one thing a scout knows, it's that you have to
"be prepared," and the kids in this troop had
everything from toothbrushes to frying pans.

Old Dog had trained his boys well. There was one, however, a bully named Nero Hogwash, who never listened. This pig considered himself smarter than scouting. He only joined the troop because his mama had insisted, hoping the scouts could shape him up. So far, this had not happened. Nero was never prepared. Nero never listened to the

scoutmaster. He gobbled up the refreshments before the meeting was over. Worst of all, he made fun of the other boys for taking scouting so seriously. But tonight, everyone was so excited about tomorrow's trip, they paid very little attention to Nero, except for a cat named Scrap who went along with Nero to avoid the ridicule of the pig.

The morning of the big trip arrived. Mama Hogwash, who ordinarily did not get up so early, dragged her hamhocks from bed and roused her sleeping pig. No matter how much Nero complained and whined, Mama Hogwash was determined to send him on this trip.

Between sips of coffee and puffs on a cigarette, she said to a friend on the telephone,

"No, he doesn't want to go. No, he doesn't appear to have scouting in his blood. But if I don't get that kid out of this house for a couple of weeks, I will go crazy!"

When his mama wasn't looking, Nero stole a cigarette from her purse. "Hee, hee, hee," Nero snickered to himself.

The scout truck arrived and Mama
Hogwash kissed Nero's snout and pushed him
out the door.

"Now you be Mama's good little pig," she
hollered, waving goodbye.

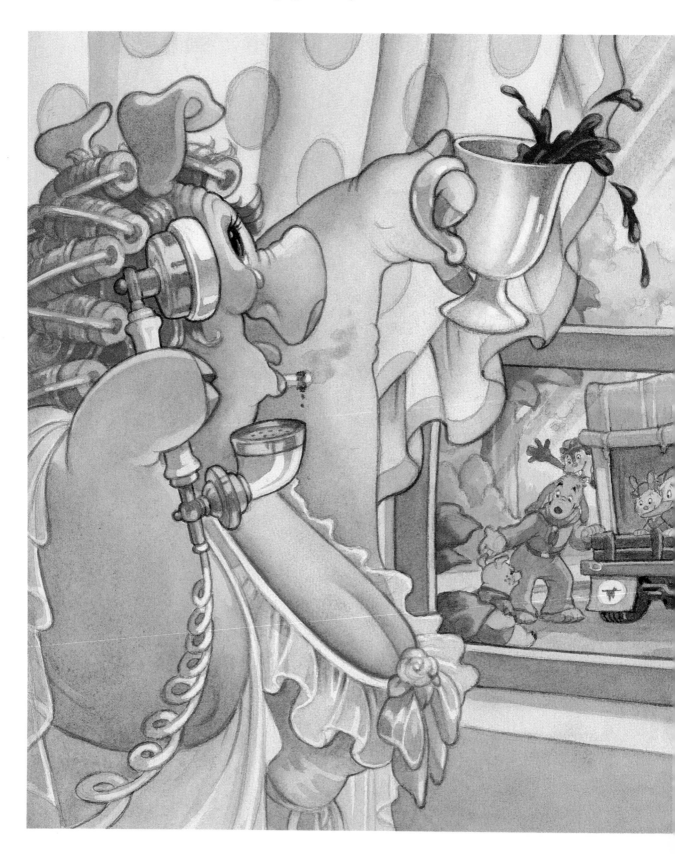

Nero Hogwash felt the stolen cigarette hidden in his pocket. "Hee, hee, hee," he chuckled, thinking he was very clever.

Old Dog helped Nero into the truck and away the scouts went.

Isn't it funny how people are different? On the one hand, the buddies loved everything about scouting and this trip was a real adventure. On the other hand, Nero Hogwash hated everything about scouting. And what's amazing, when you step back and look real close, is that the folks who resist and resent and gripe are the folks who need a thing most.

The truck rolled through the outskirts of the city and into the countryside. After many hours, the scouts left the countryside and were now pressing upward into the mountain wilderness where the scenery was totally awesome. The clean mountain breeze blew through their hair and whistled in their ears. Dickie Duck, Jack Rabbit, and Bobo could hardly contain their excitement.

"Look at the mountains! Look at the sky! Look at the trees!" they shouted.

But the pig wasn't watching the mountains, the sky, or the trees. He was stuffing his face with candy bars and tossing the wrappers out the back of the truck.

"Nero, you shouldn't do that!" Dickie Duck said.

"You're a scout and you're not supposed to litter."

Nero snorted back, "How would you like your bill bent, Duck?"

"Oh, I wouldn't!" quacked Dickie.

"Then mind your own business," grunted the pig. And for the rest of the drive, the buddies avoided the littering pig.

Finally, they arrived at the campsite. And
what a sight it was! They set up their tents in a
clearing. There was a big lake on one side
where they could fish and swim; and all
around, there were hills to climb. Nero
Hogwash convinced Scrap Cat they should
stay out of sight until the work was done.

On the other hand, Dickie, Jack, and Bobo
had been at the very center of activity. When
the campsite was all set, they went exploring
and found a poster of Smokey Bear on a tree.

Jack Rabbit read aloud, " 'Only you can
prevent forest fires.' That's a good thing to
remember," said Jack. "I read that most fires
are started because people don't think."

The buddies heard laughter behind them and turned to see Nero and Scrap Cat.

"You guys are really a bunch of jerks," sneered the pig. "All this goodie-goodie stuff, gung-ho scouts, and now Smokey Bear. When are you gonna grow up? There's no such person as Smokey Bear. That bear is just some dummy that somebody made up to try and scare kids about fires. Get real!" he continued. "See how green those trees are? Well, trees that are green don't burn!"

Bobo's instinct was to punch the pig in the snout, but his friends stopped him. After all, the pig was big and his friend Scrap Cat had razor-sharp fingernails.

"You guys stay out of my face!" Nero threatened.

"That goes for me double," snapped the cat.

Nero swaggered off to his tent with Scrap tagging along behind.

The scouts slept like logs that night in the forest. The next morning, they ate a hearty breakfast of sausages and hotcakes dripping with butter and swimming in hot maple syrup. Everything smelled and tasted so good in the fresh mountain air. Nero made a pig of himself.

Consequently, when the troop took their
hike, the fat pig was so uncomfortably stuffed
that he lagged behind, waddling and griping to
his friend, the cat. Trusty Beaver, the troop,
and the buddies strode far ahead, taking in the
wonders of this wilderness world.

The scouts hiked to the top of a cliff with a
magnificent view. Dickie, Jack, and Bobo had
never seen anything so awesome.

But hidden down in the bushes, the pig
who was "smarter than scouting" pulled out

his stolen cigarette.

Nero Hogwash wallowed in hog heaven as he sat there smoking, just like a "big pig." He even convinced Scrap Cat to take a few puffs, but it only made the cat feel a little sick.

Nero and Scrap Cat rejoined the others as they hiked back down the hill. No one would ever know their secret, or would they?

You see, Nero had left something dangerous behind — the cigarette butt. He had carelessly stepped on it only once. Now if there's one thing a scout knows, it's "Never be careless with fire." But since the pig thought he was "smarter than scouting" and did not believe in Smokey Bear, he didn't give this cigarette butt a thought. And there it lay, with a tiny orange spark glowing in its ashes — a bomb waiting to go off.

During the hike back, Nero was uncontrollable. He playfully pushed several boys, including Scrap, off the trail into some poison oak. Dickie, Jack, and Bobo stuck together and stayed away from the pig and out of harm.

By the time the troop got back to camp,
the other scouts were scratching and crying.
Trusty Beaver got out the calamine lotion,
but there wasn't enough. There was only
one thing left to do. The injured scouts
would have to be taken home.

Scoutmaster Old Dog was an extremely patient man, but Nero had pushed him too far. He pulled the boy aside and, controlling his anger, he quietly explained.

"I know you think you're 'smarter than scouting,' and maybe you think I haven't noticed what's been going on since you joined our troop. Well, I have. I haven't done anything about it because you need what we have to offer more than any of the other boys. But this time you've gone too far, so I'm sending you home with the other kids."

The pig panicked! If he came home early, Mama Hogwash would be furious. He pleaded and promised to be better. And the scoutmaster, who was always willing to help any boy who was willing to try, reconsidered and said Nero could stay.

But way down deep, in his piggy heart, Nero was plotting a way to get back at Old Dog. That night, the hog got a log and quietly dragged it to the entrance of the scoutmaster's tent.

"Hee, hee, hee," he snickered. "When that

old dummy comes out in the morning, "he'll trip and fall flat on his face. That'll show him!"

As usual, Nero was not thinking and his pranks were just about to backfire. You see, the careless bomb Nero had left in the woods had just gone off.

FIRE! FIRE! FIRE! Everywhere
green trees hissed and exploded! A wall
of flame surrounded the camp! Red hot
embers shot through the air, spreading

the fire. The uncontrolled forest fire
roared around the scout camp. If the
scouts were to survive, they had to think
and act quickly!

"Boys!" shouted the scoutmaster. "We've got to get down to the lake!"

But what was that in front of the Old Dog's tent? Oh, no! The hog log!

The scoutmaster tripped just as Nero planned and fell flat on his face! He was knocked out cold, and broke his arm with the fall. The pig hadn't learned his lesson; he was about to get burned. The fire was upon them and the one person who would know what to do was unconscious. Things looked bad. Things looked very bad.

Nero went berserk. "It's death!" he screamed, blindly running straight into the flames. His clothes caught fire. The faster the pig ran, the more he fanned the flames.

Now if there's one thing a scout knows, it's "Don't run if you are on fire. You drop to the ground and roll out the flames."

Instinctively, Bobo jumped into action. He tackled the streaking pig. With his hands, he beat out the flames.

Now you might ask yourself, "How did he know to do such a thing?" I'll tell you. He listened at the meetings and read his scout book. He never thought he'd be caught in a fire, but when he was, Bobo was prepared.

His buddies, Jack and Dickie, were also prepared. They had taken their shirts and made a stretcher just like the one in the handbook. Quickly but carefully, they lifted Old Dog on it.

If there's one thing a scout knows, it's "In the heat of confusion, keep a cool head." Without panicking, the buddies dodged the flames and headed for the lake with the burnt pig and unconscious dog.

All through the night, they stayed safe in
the water. When the scoutmaster came to, he
saw how well the boys had handled the
situation. He was very proud of them.

Nero just whimpered and cried, "I want to

go home. I want my mama."

He didn't look much like a big pig now, just a big baby. Worst of all, he was afraid someone would find out that it was he who started this forest fire.

At dawn, the firefighters had the blaze under
control. Trusty Beaver arrived with the rangers in
a rescue helicopter. Nero was in for one final shock.
Who should step out of the chopper, but Smokey
Bear! His eyes were large and kind but very serious.

"We're glad you're safe," said Smokey.
"You could have been killed."

"Thanks to my scouts here," said the scoutmaster, "we're all right."

Smokey looked at the charred waste all around him and sadly shook his head. "This was probably started by someone who didn't think. When will people ever learn? Only you can prevent forest fires."

Nero's burns were bandaged. He never told anyone about the cigarette, but he and Scrap Cat both knew. Getting burned once was enough for the cat; after that he became a model scout.

At a special awards meeting, Old Dog
publicly commended the buddies and decorated
them for bravery. The kids in the troop went
crazy, shouting and applauding their friends.

Many years have passed, and Dickie Duck, Jack Rabbit, and Bobo are now grown up and have gone their separate ways; but they frequently recall those golden days when they were scouts. Sometimes they take out their badges. Sometimes they put them on. And when they do, a strange thing happens. They are no longer grown up. They are no longer miles apart. They are once again young and the buddies.